The Divine Sister

by Charles Busch

SAMUEL FRENCH

FOUNDED 1830

NEW YORK HOLLYWOOD LONDON TORONTO

SAMUELFRENCH.COM

ISBN 978-0-573-69886-6   Printed in U.S.A.   #29657

MUSIC USE NOTE

Licensees are solely responsible for obtaining formal written permission from copyright owners to use copyrighted music in the performance of this play and are strongly cautioned to do so. If no such permission is obtained by the licensee, then the licensee must use only original music that the licensee owns and controls. Licensees are solely responsible and liable for all music clearances and shall indemnify the copyright owners of the play and their licensing agent, Samuel French, Inc., against any costs, expenses, losses and liabilities arising from the use of music by licensees.

For permission and licensing of the music to the song "Trinity of Harmony," contact the composer Lewis Flynn's agent, Corinne Hayoun at Creative Artists Agency, 162 Fifth Avenue, 6th Floor, New York, NY 10013.

IMPORTANT BILLING AND CREDIT
REQUIREMENTS

All producers of *THE DIVINE SISTER* must give credit to the Author of the Play in all programs distributed in connection with performances of the Play, and in all instances in which the title of the Play appears for the purposes of advertising, publicizing or otherwise exploiting the Play and/ or a production. The name of the Author *must* appear on a separate line on which no other name appears, immediately following the title and *must* appear in size of type not less than fifty percent of the size of the title type.

In addition the following credit *must* be given in all programs and publicity information distributed in association with this piece:

THE DIVINE SISTER was produced by Daryl Roth and Bob Boyett at Soho Playhouse in New York City on September 22, 2010.

THE DIVINE SISTER was developed at Theater For The New City (Crystal Field, Executive Artistic Director) in New York City in February, 2010.

THEATER FOR THE NEW CITY

CRYSTAL FIELD, EXECUTIVE ARTISTIC DIRECTOR,

PRESENTS

WITH THE GENEROUS SUPPORT OF

LAND LINE PRODUCTIONS, HENRY VAN AMERINGEN
& CORCORAN GROUP REAL ESTATE

THE DIVINE SISTER

WRITTEN BY AND STARRING

CHARLES BUSCH

FEATURING

| ALISON FRASER | JULIE HALSTON |
| AMY RUTBERG | JENNIFER VAN DYCK |

JONATHAN WALKER

SCENIC DESIGNER	LIGHTING DESIGNER	COSTUME DESIGNER	SOUND DESIGNER
B.T. WHITEHILL	KIRK BOOKMAN	FABIO TOBLINI	JILL BC DUBOFF

ORIGINAL MUSIC	WIG DESIGNER	PHOTOGRAPHER
LEWIS FLINN	KATHERINE CARR	DAVID RODGERS

COMPANY MANAGER	PRODUCTION STAGE MANAGER	PRESS
DANIELLE KARLINER	ANGELA ALLEN	AARON MEIER

DIRECTED BY

CARL ANDRESS

SOHO PLAYHOUSE

Darren Lee Cole & Faith Mulvihill, *Executive Directors*

Daryl Roth & Bob Boyett
PRESENT

Charles Busch
STARRING IN HIS HOLY OUTRAGEOUS NEW COMEDY

ᵗʰᴱ DivineSister

FEATURING

Alison Fraser Amy Rutberg
Jennifer Van Dyck Jonathan Walker
AND **Julie Halston**

SCENIC/GRAPHIC DESIGNER	COSTUME DESIGNER	LIGHTING DESIGNER	SOUND DESIGNER
B.T. Whitehill	**Fabio Toblini**	**Kirk Bookman**	**Jill BC DuBoff**

WIG DESIGN BY	ORIGINAL MUSIC BY
Katherine Carr	**Lewis Flinn**

PRESS	STRATEGIC MARKETING	ONLINE MARKETING
Boneau/Bryan-Brown	**aka**	**Pit Bull Interactive**

PRODUCTION STAGE MANAGER	PRODUCTION MANAGER	COMPANY MANAGER
Angela Allen	**Ricardo Taylor**	**Danielle Karliner**

GENERAL MANAGER	ASSOCIATE PRODUCERS
Adam Hess	**Alexander Fraser Tim Levy**
	Land Line Productions

DIRECTED BY

Carl Andress

The producers wish to express their appreciation to
Theatre Development Fund for its support of this production.

CAST
(in alphabetical order)

Mother Superior ....CHARLES BUSCH

Sister Walburga/Mrs. Macduffie ....ALISON FRASER

Sister Acacius ....JULIE HALSTON

Agnes ....AMY RUTBERG

Mrs. Levinson/Timothy ....JENNIFER VAN DYCK

Jeremy/Brother Venerius ....JONATHAN WALKER

STANDBYS
Standbys never substitute for the listed performers
unless a specific announcement is made at the time of the appearance.
For Mother Superior, Sister Walburga/Mrs. Macduffie, Jeremy/Brother Venerius—DAVID
DRAKE; for Sister Walburga/Mrs. Macduffie, Sister Acacius, Agnes, Mrs.
Levinson/Timothy—MARCY McGUIGAN.

Production Stage Manager—ANGELA ALLEN
Assistant Stage Manager—TRISHA HENSON

CHARACTERS

AGNES
SISTER WALBURGA
MRS. MACDUFFIE
SISTER ACACIUS AKA LIL
MOTHER SUPERIOR AKA SUSAN
MRS. LEVINSON
TIMOTHY
JEREMY
BROTHER VENERIUS

DOUBLE CASTING

Please note that the actor who plays Sister Walburg also plays Mrs. MacDuffie, the actor who plays Mrs. Levinson also plays Timothy, and the actor who plays Jeremy also plays Brother Venerius.

Scene One

(Pittsburgh, April 1966. St. Veronica's convent school. The school courtyard. **SISTER MARIA WALBURGA,** *a severe doctrinarian from the mother house in Berlin, has just arrived and is being given a tour by the ethereal young postulant,* **AGNES.***)*

AGNES. The children are all in class, Sister Maria Walburga. A rare moment of peace at St. Veronica's. I'm sure your school in Germany has its fair share of rambunctious little dumplings.

WALBURGA. Ach du lieber. Dieses mädchen ist ein Einfaltspinsel. *(trans: Oy, this girl is a nincompoop.)*

AGNES. On the other side of this courtyard was once the children's playground. The Sisters were forced to sell the lot to save the school from closing. It breaks my heart to see the children denied the freedom to play. It breaks my heart.

WALBURGA. Bah! Sentimental rubbish. *(with a deeply suspicious air)* Nonetheless, this news disturbs me. This institution appears to be in severe financial trouble.

AGNES. The building itself is falling apart. Last year, I am told, one of the Sisters was decapitated by a crumbling cornice. But I'm sure she and her head are far happier now in God's bosom.

WALBURGA. How long have you been at St. Veronica's?

AGNES. Only a few months. I arrived on January 17, 1966. I now consider that the day I was born.

WALBURGA. Where did you come from?

AGNES. Here in Pittsburgh. I've never lived anywhere else. I do love it so. There is something dark and grotesque in this city that I find a comfort.

WALBURGA. Child, you seem queer.

AGNES. Do I, Sister?

WALBURGA. Your eyes betray that you may be hiding something.

AGNES. Oh, but I am not, Sister. There is nothing behind my eyes.

WALBURGA. There is no room for secrets in the religious life.

AGNES. Perhaps what you observe is that I have saintly visions, hear heavenly voices and have the power to heal. But that's all.

(**SISTER ACACIUS** *enters - a hearty, athletic gal; she speaks with a pronounced New Yawk accent.*)

ACACIUS. There you are. This is the limit! This time you have really gone too far! *(notices* **SISTER WALBURGA***)* Oh my, you must be Sister Maria Walburga. Direct from the Deutschland. Have you been here long? I'm Sister Acacius.

WALBURGA. I have only just arrived. And your position at St. Veronica's?

ACACIUS. As we are both a convent and a grade school, I act as Mistress of Novices and wrestling coach. In fact, most of the kids lovingly refer to me as Coach Acacius.

WALBURGA. That sounds suspiciously secular. The postulant was kind enough to provide me with a brief tour.

ACACIUS. Sister, don't get the idea that this girl is typical of our order. We're not all kooks and oddballs.

WALBURGA. The postulant was just telling me about her sacred powers.

ACACIUS. Powers? This girl needs evaluation and treatment for a mental disorder.

AGNES. I only tell what I hear and what I see.

ACACIUS. You're testing my patience.

WALBURGA. Child, describe to me your visions.

ACACIUS. Visions. Ha! We wasted a perfectly good rhubarb pie because she claimed she saw in it the face of Thomas Aquinas. Go on. Tell Sister Walburga about your latest vision. Get a load of this.

WALBURGA. Tell me, child.

AGNES. This morning, I was working in the laundry. I was scrubbing one of the boys' underpants upon which I saw the holy face of St. Clare.

ACACIUS. Etched among the urine stains. This is sacrilege!

(AGNES takes the heavily stained underpants out of her pocket and shows SISTER WALBURGA.)

AGNES. Sister Maria Walburga, do you not see the delicate features of St. Clare?

WALBURGA. I see the door to the Burgemeister's Office in Düsseldorf.

ACACIUS. Those urine stains are a Rorschach test. You see what you want to see.

AGNES. It is the face of St. Clare. It is.

ACACIUS. You're a pathological liar!

WALBURGA. Sister, control yourself!

ACACIUS. Only those who've endured great torment can gaze upon the divine. I know what it is to suffer. Look at my eyes. They burn like the very fires of Hell. Why? Because they need sleep. They need rest, which I will not give them. My throat is parched from constant prayer. My hands are gnarled from serving God in humiliation. How can you who have never felt pain dare to say you are the chosen one? WHY NOT ME?!!!!

AGNES. Sister, I don't know why I was chosen. You are a hundred times more worthy.

ACACIUS. Aw, shut your hole. Here comes Mother Superior.

(MOTHER SUPERIOR enters on her bicycle. She fairly glows with serene lovliness and yet is infused with boundless energy and toughness of spirit.)

MOTHER SUPERIOR. Clear the tarmac, Sisters! We're heading for a landing! *(dismounts)* Ah, you must be Sister Maria Walburga. Welcome to St. Veronica's. As you can see, Pittsburgh's reputation as a bleak, industrial metropolis is not quite deserved. Notice if you will, not a cloud in the sky. The hollyhocks are in bloom. The lilacs. The forsythia. Agnes, posture. Tell me, Sister, how are things at the Mother House in Berlin?

WALBURGA. We are thriving and moving ever forward. Your school appears to be on its way towards extinction.

MOTHER SUPERIOR. True, our vows of poverty have been tested, but like the rock of St. Peter, St. Veronica's shall endure.

WALBURGA. The Mother Abbess in Berlin has told me that you have petitioned for the right to tear down the present building.

MOTHER SUPERIOR. Yes, to build a new modern one in its place. Oh, there's the usual bunch of liberal naysayers who claim the building is worthy of preservation. Lincoln spoke here. Rare gothic details. Historic mosaics. I say, "Blow it up and don't look back."

WALBURGA. Reverend Mother, I trust St. Veronica's can survive your postulant's claims of holy visions and healing powers.

MOTHER SUPERIOR. So you've heard. My child, I thought we had resolved this matter.

ACACIUS. She's been up to her same shenanigans. Show Reverend Mother the underpants in question.

(AGNES shows her the briefs.)

MOTHER SUPERIOR. I don't think I quite understand.

ACACIUS. Do the pee stains form any sort of image to you?

MOTHER SUPERIOR. Let's see. It could be a hippopotamus. JFK in profile. What exactly am I looking for?

AGNES. The sorrowful face of the blessed St. Clare.

MOTHER SUPERIOR. Agnes, Agnes, you gave me your solemn promise that this would never happen again.

AGNES. I tried but when the Saints ask me to spread their word, I cannot refuse.

ACACIUS. This insubordination must not be tolerated.

WALBURGA. Such rebellion will have to be reported to the Mother House.

MOTHER SUPERIOR. I don't think we need bother the Mother House. My children, the postulant is adjusting to the religious life. We must be patient. Acacius, has the church not been tolerant of your own rebellious nature?

ACACIUS. I never claimed to heal people. If this gets around, we'll have all of Pittsburgh and half of Altoona lined up down the block.

MOTHER SUPERIOR. Child, who have you healed lately?

AGNES. Well, I cured Sister Ann of her sciatica and Sister Bernard's stuttering.

MOTHER SUPERIOR. Ten bucks if you can cure Father Fogarty's flatulence.

ACACIUS. Reverend Mother, this is not something that should be treated lightly –

MOTHER SUPERIOR. Enough. Sisters, this is no time for us to be distracted with internal strife. Our very walls are crumbling about us. I have forged a plan. Acacius, this afternoon you and I shall visit the home of the distinguished philanthropist, Mrs. Morris Levinson.

WALBURGA. Levinson? She sounds like a Jew.

MOTHER SUPERIOR. Yes, I believe she is a Jewess, but we must not condemn her personally for the murder of our Savior. Others? Perhaps. Acacius, why don't you bring Sister Walburga with you to your wrestling class? She looks like she could give the kids some pointers.

WALBURGA. Reverend Mother, we shall speak later in private.

(**MOTHER SUPERIOR** *notices* **AGNES** *staring transfixed at the underpants.*)

MOTHER SUPERIOR. Agnes, perhaps it's best if we let Sister Acacius hold on to the controversial bvd's.

AGNES. Yes, Reverend Mother.

WALBURGA. Auf Wiedersehen, Reverend Mother.

(**MOTHER SUPERIOR** *hands them to* **SISTER ACACIUS,** *who bows and exits with* **WALBURGA**.)

MOTHER SUPERIOR. Child, child, child. What am I to do with you? I believe your vocation to be a true one but I cannot allow my convent to become a battleground.

AGNES. Reverend Mother, I'm sorry to have caused you concern. You have been so kind to me.

MOTHER SUPERIOR. We have much in common. We both lost our parents in infancy. You were lucky enough to have been adopted. And yes, my early years in the convent were also fraught with rebellion. To eliminate vanity has been my perpetual struggle.

(*She lifts her face up beatifically into a flattering key light.*)

AGNES. Did you always know you would be a nun?

MOTHER SUPERIOR. Goodness, no. When I was young, my great dream was to be a newspaper reporter. And I had a real flair for it. Grabbing a hot story from the editor's desk and being the first to arrive at the murder scene. Snapping photos. Getting the scoop while the coppers were still scratching their b– heads.

AGNES. Was it painful giving all that up?

MOTHER SUPERIOR. I found something better.

AGNES. But certainly not as exciting.

MOTHER SUPERIOR. I find God exciting. My dear, we are living in a time of great social change. We must do everything in our power to stop it. It is in our hands to save mankind from the atheists, the adulterers, the homosexuals, the communists, the Dave Clark Five. Yes, indeed, these are fascinating times. My dear Agnes, Live! Live! Live! Life is a banquet and most poor suckers haven't even said "grace."

AGNES. I suppose I don't appreciate the world around me.

MOTHER SUPERIOR. It's the simple things that make life worthwhile. Raindrops on daisies, whiskers on old women, bright copper pennies and hiking and swimmin'. And of course, music. I derive great pleasure from music of every kind. Well, not every kind. Real music. White people's music. Dear, would you fetch my guitar from behind the Virgin?

(**AGNES** *brings over the guitar that was behind the Altar of the Virgin Mary.* **MOTHER SUPERIOR** *begins to strum.*)

AGNES. I didn't know you played the guitar.

MOTHER SUPERIOR. Oh yes, I taught myself as a lonely child in the orphanage. When I strum my guitar and raise my voice in song, that's when I do believe I feel closest to "him."

(She sings:)

LA LA LA, LA LA LA, LA LA
A SONG WITHOUT WORDS
A MELODY FROM THE HEART
THREE NOTES FORM A CHORD
WHICH BRINGS US CLOSER TO THE LORD

THREE SIMPLE NOTES. "LA LA LA"
A TRINITY OF HARMONY
SING HA-LAY-LOO-YAH!

LA LA LA, LA LA LA
LA LA LA, LA LA LA

SAINT EUNICE WAS NAILED TO A PINE DOOR
SAINT BLANDINA WAS MUNCHED BY A WILD BOAR
SAINT BLANCHE WAS GOUGED FOR A FAUX PAS
BUT ALL THE WHILE THEY SANG "LA, LA, LA"

(spoken) Sing with me Agnes. It stimulates the corpuscles!

AGNES. *(spoken)* I'll try!

> *(Both sing:)*
> A SONG WITHOUT WORDS
> A MELODY FROM THE HEART
> THREE NOTES FORM A CHORD
> WHICH BRINGS US CLOSER TO THE LORD
> THREE SIMPLE NOTES "LA, LA, LA"
> A TRINITY OF HARMONY
> SING HA-LAY-LOO-YAH!

MOTHER. LA LA LA

AGNES.   (LA, LA, LA)

MOTHER. LA LA LA

AGNES.   (LA, LA, LA)

MOTHER. LA LA LA

AGNES.   (LA, LA, LA)

BOTH. LA LA LA

MOTHER. SAINT SEBASTIAN WAS PIERCED BY ARROWS

AGNES.   SAINT HARVEY'S EYES WERE PLUCKED OUT BY
                   SPARROWS

MOTHER. SAINT BALDRIC'S DEATH WAS HARDLY A "HA HA HA"

AGNES.   BUT HEARTILY

BOTH. HE SANG "LA, LA, LA!"

MOTHER. A SONG WITHOUT WORDS

AGNES   (A SONG WITHOUT WORDS)

MOTHER. A MELODY FROM THE HEART

AGNES.   (A MELODY FROM THE HEART)

MOTHER. THREE NOTES FORM A CHORD

AGNES.   (THREE NOTES FORM A CHORD)

MOTHER. WHICH BRINGS US CLOSER TO THE LORD

AGNES.   (THE LORD)

MOTHER. THREE SIMPLE NOTES "LA, LA, LA"

> A TRINITY

BOTH. OF HARMONY

> SING "RAH, RAH, RAH!"

MOTHER. LA LA LA

AGNES.   (LA, LA, LA)

MOTHER. LA LA LA

AGNES.   (LA, LA, LA)

MOTHER. LA LA LA

AGNES.   (LA, LA, LA)

BOTH. LA LA LA

    LA LA LA, LA LA LA

    LA LA LA, LA LA LA, LA, LA!!

MOTHER. A TRINITY OF HARMONY

AGNES.   (A TRINITY OF HARMONY)

BOTH. SING HA-LAY-LOO-YAH!

(SISTER ACACIUS enters.)

ACACIUS. Reverend Mother.

MOTHER SUPERIOR. Yes, Acacius.

ACACIUS. I'm afraid there's been an unfortunate accident. On my way to the gymnasium, I slipped and dropped the underpants down the well.

(She takes the wrung out underpants out of her habit.)

At least, the stains have been removed.

(AGNES begins to tremble and moan. Her eyes roll up into her head.)

MOTHER SUPERIOR. My dear. My dear.

(AGNES looks up at some unseen face. She appears to glow from within.)

AGNES. Yes. Yes. I see you. So beautiful. I love you. I love you.

ACACIUS. Reverend Mother, look at her hands. Look at her hands!

(Both of AGNES's palms are bleeding.)

AGNES. *(sobbing)* It won't stop! The blood. His blood. The blood of my Lord!

(MOTHER SUPERIOR examines her hand and discovers something.)

MOTHER SUPERIOR. What is this?

ACACIUS. What are you blind? It's stigmata!

MOTHER SUPERIOR. It's a maraschino cherry. Child?

AGNES. *(sheepishly)* Oh, I'm sorry. I forgot I stole some cherries off of Sister Benedict's birthday cake.

MOTHER SUPERIOR. Agnes!

End of Scene

Scene Two

(A dark secret room underneath the convent. **SISTER WALBURGA** *enters carrying a lantern. She looks for someone.)*

WALBURGA. Brother Venerius, are you here?

(From out of the shadows comes a frightening figure: **BROTHER VENERIUS,** *a sinister Albino monk.)*

VENERIUS. I am with you, Sister.

WALBURGA. This underground chamber took me longer to find than I anticipated. None of the other sisters knows of its existence.

VENERIUS. Sister, you are not what I expected.

WALBURGA. And just what were you expecting, Brother Venerius?

VENERIUS. I was told very little from our contact in Germany. I could only rely on my somewhat overzealous imagination.

WALBURGA. Remember these words: I am not what I seem.

VENERIUS. You do know the importance of your mission? We are here to protect nothing less than the course of history.

WALBURGA. Have you the code that reveals to us what to expect in the future?

VENERIUS. The code is in the form of an epigram deconstructed as an anagram written as a cryptogram in the shape of a hexagram.

WALBURGA. But what does it mean?

VENERIUS. That code was merely a smokescreen to disguise the true code which is imbedded in the cloak worn in Botticelli's painting of the Birth of Venus in the Uffizzi Gallery in Florence. Four brilliant Russian dwarves were sent to break that code.

WALBURGA. And what did it say?

VENERIUS. Each of the dwarves was found murdered in a different foreign capital with eight letters in its name. You take the second and fifth letter of each city, put them together and then look at the message in a bathroom mirror.

WALBURGA. And what does it say?

VENERIUS. All I can reveal is that "she" is here.

WALBURGA. Close?

VENERIUS. Very close.

WALBURGA. Yes, I can feel her presence. I can smell the perfume of her being.

VENERIUS. I am sure she can hear our every word.

WALBURGA. Our every prayer.

VENERIUS. Sister, I will lay down my life to protect her. I am prepared to kill any infidel who brings her harm.

WALBURGA. Yes, yes, kill, kill. Kill to protect her. That is why I was sent for and I shall not disappoint.

VENERIUS. If you fail at your task, nothing less than the entire future of the world is at stake.

WALBURGA. I shall not fail.

End of Scene

Scene Three

(A street in the fashionable part of town. **MOTHER SUPERIOR** *and* **SISTER ACACIUS** *are on their way to visit Mrs. Levinson.* **SISTER ACACIUS** *is moving faster.)*

ACACIUS. Reverend Mother, am I walking too fast? You know me and my strong, healthy stride.

MOTHER SUPERIOR. I was listening to the melody of the Robin Red Breast. God gives all of his creatures perfect pitch, if they'd only sing with hearts full of prayer.

ACACIUS. Reverend Mother, I just hear a lot of squawkin'.

MOTHER SUPERIOR. Acacius, I know you have a true appreciation of our Lord's wonders. Can't you smell the fragrant perfume of his fir trees?

ACACIUS. My sniffer tells me a lot of poodles have been walked on this fancy block. *(looking down)* And evidently a Great Dane.

MOTHER SUPERIOR. No, spring is in the air. I had so hoped we'd be further along in our fundraising efforts before the celebration of our Savior's resurrection.

ACACIUS. You nervous, Mother?

MOTHER SUPERIOR. Yes, very. And full of doubt. Yes, doubt. With my every prayer, I ask the King of Kings in all humility; do I have the courage and fortitude to lead St. Veronica's into the modern world?

ACACIUS. That's crazy talk. Reverend Mother, never forget, you're a heavyweight. You've gone to the mat many times for the Lord and always scored a knockout.

MOTHER SUPERIOR. My dear Acacius, I'm not sure his Holiness in Rome would approve of your sports lingo, but I won't sell you short to the Commission. Oh, my dear friend, in the great scheme of things, my accomplishments seem quite insignificant.

ACACIUS. Are you kidding? Say, didn't we sandbag that tight-fisted publisher, Mr. Fishbaum, into donating all them math books?

MOTHER SUPERIOR. True, and we squeezed marching band uniforms out of that grouchy manufacturer, Mr. Blechman.

ACACIUS. And how's about when we sucker punched that rag trade tycoon, Mr. Plotnick, for football jerseys?

MOTHER SUPERIOR. I hope we're as successful with Mrs. Levinson. The lady's known for her generous philanthropy. She must be very close to God.

ACACIUS. Reverend Mother, give us one round in the ring with her. She'll be down for the count and won't even know what hit her.

MOTHER SUPERIOR. Ah, that must be her house at the end of the block. Sister, do let's hurry.

(With renewed vigor, they quicken their pace.)

End of Scene

Scene Four

(The sitting room in the grand mansion belonging to Mrs. Morris Levinson. **MRS. LEVINSON**, *an imposing and elegant matriarch, is reluctantly receiving* **MOTHER SUPERIOR** *and* **SISTER ACACIUS**.*)*

MRS. LEVINSON. Good afternoon, Sisters. I must say, this is the first time I have welcomed nuns into my drawing room.

MOTHER SUPERIOR. And a most grand and impressive drawing room it is, Mrs. Levinson. I suppose you would more likely be receiving your Rabbi.

MRS. LEVINSON. That would also be highly unlikely. Sisters, what can I do for you?

ACACIUS. She gets to the point. I like her.

MOTHER SUPERIOR. The profound tradition of Jewish philanthropy has led us to your gate.

MRS. LEVINSON. I imagine you wish to secure a sizeable donation from me.

MOTHER SUPERIOR. You are a wise soul, Widow Levinson. Is she not, Sister Acacius?

ACACIUS. The lady's got our number.

MRS. LEVINSON. Well, I am sorry to disappoint you, Sisters, but my charitable donations for the year have already been dispersed.

MOTHER SUPERIOR. Widow Levinson, may we be frank? St. Veronica's shall soon be no more. We are in search of a miracle. Miracle. How would you say that in Yiddish?

MRS. LEVINSON. I haven't the foggiest idea. In any case, I am afraid I cannot help you.

MOTHER SUPERIOR. You must not be, shall we say, unfamiliar with the bitter gall of poverty. I can see you as a young girl in the shtetl, grinding with a mortar and pestle your gefilte fish for the evening's Sabbath.

MRS. LEVINSON. You are most presumptuous. I hail from generations of aristocracy. My grandfather was presented at the court of Queen Victoria.

ACACIUS. But I bet you still enjoy a good kosher pickle.

MRS. LEVINSON. How dare you.

MOTHER SUPERIOR. Widow Levinson –

MRS. LEVINSON. And do not call me "Widow Levinson."

MOTHER SUPERIOR. But as a Jew –

MRS. LEVINSON. Let me make one thing perfectly clear before I escort you both to the door. I have no religious affiliations, nor did my father or his father before him. I am a confirmed atheist.

MOTHER SUPERIOR. *(shuddering)* Are you telling me that you do not believe in God?

MRS. LEVINSON. I believe God in all of its manifestations, be it Jewish, Catholic, Buddhist or whatever, is a fairy tale created by men to pacify them on their fear of death.

ACACIUS. But when things go wrong, you don't ever shoot a quick prayer to you know who?

MRS. LEVINSON. Absolutely not. In fact, each year I lend considerable financial support to the World Atheist Consortium, the National Organization of Atheists and the Atheist Society of Greater Allegheny. I've also established the Margaret Levinson Scholarship for Young Atheists, the Margaret Levinson Foundation for Middle-aged Free Thinkers and the Margaret Levinson Center for Senior Non-believers.

MOTHER SUPERIOR. Well, I'm pleased we of the Church have given you something to believe in.

MRS. LEVINSON. I have found contentment in this life through my love for my late husband, something you wouldn't know about.

MOTHER SUPERIOR. Oh, but I do love a very unique and wonderful man.

MRS. LEVINSON. I beg your pardon. Whoever could that be?

MOTHER SUPERIOR. A carpenter's son from Galilee. And he's quite a guy.

MRS. LEVINSON. Extraordinary.

ACACIUS. He's my man, too, but there's plenty of him to go around.

MRS. LEVINSON. This has been most enlightening. If you'll excuse me, I have many things to attend to.

MOTHER SUPERIOR. Mrs. Levinson, now that you are widowed, do you not find this enormous house terribly lonely?

MRS. LEVINSON. What are you driving at?

MOTHER SUPERIOR. I ask you, does one person really require fifty rooms?

MRS. LEVINSON. You want this house for your school.

ACACIUS. And convent. You wouldn't believe the conditions we live in. A leper's cave is more commodious.

MRS. LEVINSON. And where would you have *me* live? Above the dry goods store?

MOTHER SUPERIOR. Pardon me for saying this, but you don't seem very happy.

MRS. LEVINSON. Happiness is not of paramount importance to me.

MOTHER SUPERIOR. No doubt you've traveled extensively. You've dined at the most elegant of restaurants. You wear the finest of Paris fashions, and yet, nothing brings you joy. Why not try God?

MRS. LEVINSON. Reverend Mother, those robes do not grant you permission to be rude. However, as mistress of this house, I am permitted to throw you out.

MOTHER SUPERIOR. We shall leave you to your solitude but do give our plight further thought. And for your generous time, allow me to give you this St. Genesius medal. *(She takes the small medal out of her habit.)*

MRS. LEVINSON. No, thank you. Now please go.

ACACIUS. Perhaps this rosary. *(She takes a rosary out of her habit.)*

MRS. LEVINSON. Go!

MOTHER SUPERIOR. A mezuzah? *(She takes a mezuzah out of her habit.)*

MRS. LEVINSON. Get out!

(The two **SISTER***s exit, leaving* **MRS. LEVINSON** *angry and breathless.* **JEREMY***, a handsome, virile man in his forties enters.)*

JEREMY. I heard shouting. Margaret, are you all right?

MRS. LEVINSON. Those dreadful nuns.

JEREMY. Nuns?

MRS. LEVINSON. Yes, nuns. I was just attacked by the Mother Superior of St. Veronica's convent school and her demented sidekick.

JEREMY. What did they want from you?

MRS. LEVINSON. Nothing very much. Only the roof over my head. This Mother Superior had the nerve to demand that I donate my home as a replacement for her school. The house I've lived in for over forty years!

JEREMY. *(smiles to himself)* Mother Superior.

MRS. LEVINSON. You smile. You've never crossed her path.

JEREMY. Oh, but I have and should like to again. Margaret, when you graciously invited me as your houseguest, you didn't ask why I was coming to Pittsburgh.

MRS. LEVINSON. I was delighted to have the company and felt no need to pry.

JEREMY. The film company I work for very much wants to purchase the screen rights to the story of a young postulant cloistered at St. Veronica's.

MRS. LEVINSON. Really?

JEREMY. It's been kept quiet up till now, but it's said that this young girl has miraculous healing powers.

MRS. LEVINSON. Oh dear, these hysterical young girls are always ultimately exposed as fakes. Leave the child be.

JEREMY. I'm afraid I can't. When this thing pops, every film company will be vying for the rights to her story. The only way I can meet the girl is through the auspices of the Mother Superior. So far she hasn't answered any of our letters. Tomorrow I'm planning to camp out on her doorstep.

MRS. LEVINSON. Let me warn you, she is a religious fanatic.

JEREMY. That must have been quite a tea party. Were you never a believer?

MRS. LEVINSON. Not for a moment.

JEREMY. Not even an agnostic?

MRS. LEVINSON. Save me from Agnostics. Wishy washy fools afraid to take an intelligent stand. Give me the religious zealots. At least you can depend on their stupidity.

JEREMY. Did your husband share your "beliefs?"

MRS. LEVINSON. My husband, Morris, was an explorer and surprisingly, a man of faith. To prove to me the existence of God, he took me on a voyage to the ancient Island of Crete. We traveled to the dark corner of the island, far away from any tourists. I wore a Bill Blass safari jacket with a stand up collar and matching slacks. Morris wanted me to observe the life cycle of the species Sepia Officinalis, otherwise known as the cuttle fish. Yes, I saw them hatched from their mothers, small yet sinister creatures with eight arms and two tentacles. Their shells iridescent and jewel-like. Did you know that the large, staring black eyes of the cuttle fish are fully developed before birth, allowing them to hunt their prey even before hatching? And hunt their prey they did. I saw them move together as one as they stalked and ultimately devoured a terrified octopus, its ink spreading through the water in grim black floating sentences. I said, "Morris, take me away from here. I have seen enough." "No, Margaret, we must stay. We must stay. We must now see them die to feed the more superior species." And so we stayed. I removed my jacket and slacks, revealing a Schiaparelli pink bathing suit. We saw the great dolphin leap from the sea and snatch a generation of cuttle fish into its hideous gaping mouth. Morris shouted, "We are looking at the face of God! It is His will to create such divine perfection." I replied, "If that is your God, then He is a cruel one and I'll have none of Him." We returned to our hotel in silence. With an over powering dread of the unknown, I slipped into a turquoise silk Galanos. I found Morris standing on our balcony, hypnotized by the sea. And then, without a warning, he grasped his heart and fell to the ground. I knew at that very instant he was dead. And now, when I look upon the ocean, despite its glorious magnitude, all I see is debris, debris, debris. An endless trail of debris. Is that an answer to your question?

JEREMY. I forgot. What was the question?

MRS. LEVINSON. *(amused)* Then I shan't remind you. But my young friend, do beware of nuns with the eyes of a Sepia Officinalis.

JEREMY. Mother Superior wasn't always a fanatic. She was really quite different.

MRS. LEVINSON. That is a most provocative statement.

JEREMY. You see, I knew her years ago, before she entered the convent. Her name was Susan. Susan Appleyard. Girl reporter. We worked for rival newspapers in New York.

MRS. LEVINSON. She must have been a terror.

JEREMY. No. There was never a kid with more heart and gumption.

MRS. LEVINSON. You were in love with her.

JEREMY. Very much so. We met at a murder site. Susan and I were the first reporters to arrive outside the apartment house. The police wouldn't let us near the place.

(Flashback to 1946. **MOTHER SUPERIOR,** *then a vivacious redhead named* **SUSAN,** *enters.)*

JEREMY. You see anything back there?

SUSAN. Nope. The cops are as close together as gin bottles in an old maid's pantry.

JEREMY. One of them coppers just spilled that there's no evidence of a break in.

SUSAN. Just what I thought, a double suicide.

JEREMY. Have you talked to anyone who knew the kids?

SUSAN. The old lady in the apartment next door.

JEREMY. I got the girl's boss at the book shop. How's about we collaborate?

SUSAN. How's about we don't?

JEREMY. We share our sources and we both end up heroes.

SUSAN. Sorry, fella, but the dame next door has seen a lot more than the geezer in the book shop.

(The following twelve lines are overlapped.)

JEREMY. I'm pretty big stuff at the Trib. I can do things for you.

SUSAN. I bet you can. But I'm doing just fine the way I am.

JEREMY. Introduce you to the right kinds of people. How much are they paying you at the Daily Graphic?

SUSAN. Daily Mirror.

JEREMY. Sixty a week? A girl like you shouldn't be living on sixty a week.

SUSAN. Who blabbed it was sixty?

JEREMY. I bet I could get you seventy. Seventy-five if you're on the ball.

SUSAN. Seventy? My, my, my my.

JEREMY. You're the type who should be draped in furs.

SUSAN. Seventy-five? Do I hear eighty?

JEREMY. Seen ringside at the swankiest nightclubs in town. Opening night at the opera.

SUSAN. Brother, I'd quit while I was ahead. Ringside, eh? Do I hear ninety? Traviata has always been a favorite. Ah, we're up to a hundred. Going once. Going twice.

JEREMY. You scratch my back and I'll scratch yours. I'd probably be your boss but I'm a democratic sort of fellow.

SUSAN. Sold to the gentleman with the green tie.

(Overlapping ends.)

JEREMY. How does a kid like you get to be such a cynic? Was your Pa a newspaper man?

SUSAN. Nope. Never knew my folks. Grew up in an orphan-age. Learned at any early age, if you don't grab that new pair of shoes, somebody else will.

(SUSAN's best friend, LILY, runs on. She's SISTER ACA-CIUS in her earlier life.)

LILY. Susie! Susie! Wait till you get a load of this. Forget the crime of passion angle.

SUSAN. Ixnay. Ixnay.

JEREMY. Another girl reporter, eh?

LILY. Not on your life. I'm her leg man.

JEREMY. And quite a pair of legs.

SUSAN. Lily's my best friend. We room together. She's a press agent for prizefighters and wrestlers.

LILY. I get their names in Winchell. They teach me how to give a good right hook.

SUSAN. She keeps her nose to the ground and digs out all sorts of goodies for me.

JEREMY. So what's your scoop?

SUSAN. Button up, Lil. Handsome writes for the Tribune.

JEREMY. Hey, girls, give a working stiff a break?

LILY. Sorry. We girls stick together. Susie, I've gotta run. One of my fighters is on a toot. Gotta chain him to his bed before he lands himself in the jug. I'll fill you in on your so called double suicide when you get back to the apartment. One clue. The Landlord had a second set of keys. Nice meetin' ya, Slim. See ya, Susie.

(LILY exits.)

JEREMY. I like your friend.

SUSAN. Heart of solid platinum.

JEREMY. So you've got it in that pretty head to be a girl reporter.

SUSAN. I like lifting a rock and seeing what's creeping and crawling underneath.

JEREMY. You're not scared at what you'll discover?

SUSAN. Truth doesn't frighten me. Only lies.

JEREMY. Have you been lied to?

SUSAN. I couldn't trust my parents. They gave me up days after I was born.

(He kisses her.)

SUSAN. That felt nice but why did you do it?

JEREMY. It was an honest, truthful kiss. No ulterior motive.

SUSAN. Shall we delve deeper into the investigation?

(They kiss again.)

Judas Priest, the cop's left the back door unguarded.

(She kicks him in the shins.)

JEREMY. Ow!

SUSAN. Kid, it's each man for herself.

(SUSAN runs off, beating him to the scoop. The flashback ends. We are back in the present in MRS. LEVINSON's parlor.)

JEREMY. That was the beginning of beautiful romance.

MRS. LEVINSON. You're still in love with her. Aren't you?

JEREMY. It was many years ago.

MRS. LEVINSON. You will find her greatly changed.

JEREMY. I can't imagine I won't see some glimmer of that young girl.

MRS. LEVINSON. We are all haunted by memories of lost love.

JEREMY. You have regrets?

MRS. LEVINSON. What thinking person hasn't? But alas, one must abide by the choices one has made. No matter how foolish.

End of Scene

Scene Five

(The convent courtyard. **SISTER ACACIUS, SISTER WALBURGA** *and* **AGNES** *walk in a circle, silently reading from their bibles. One of them emits a dainty fart. They all surreptitiously look at each other. The guilty one pretends it's someone else. They continue walking in a circle. Another delicate fart is heard but once more no one comes forth. The church bells peal and the time for prayer is over.* **ACACIUS** *gestures to* **AGNES** *that she can go.* **AGNES** *curtsies and leaves.* **SISTER WALBURGA** *continues reading her bible. A vulnerable and sexually frustrated* **SISTER ACACIUS** *is in a chatty mood.)*

ACACIUS. Sister Walburga, have you adjusted to your new life here at St. Veronica's?

WALBURGA. *(without looking up)* Ja.

ACACIUS. I know it can be difficult starting over in a new place.

WALBURGA. Ja.

ACACIUS. Years ago, I spent a very lonely autumn in Nova Scotia. If you ever need a friendly ear, please feel free to come into my cell at any time. It's not healthy to let things fester.

*(***WALBURGA** *is intrigued and finally looks up.)*

WALBURGA. That is most generous of you, Sister.

ACACIUS. *(tremulously)* I-I-I just wouldn't want you to feel you have no friends. I'm sure if you were conversing in your native tongue you would most likely be a very gregarious, fun and outgoing person. I would imagine back in the mother house in Berlin, you had close relations with some of the other sisters.

WALBURGA. Extremely close.

ACACIUS. I've never been to Berlin, but I've heard tales. Oh boy. Have I heard tales.

WALBURGA. *(like a cat with a mouse)* What have you heard?

ACACIUS. Y'know, stuff.

WALBURGA. You must tell me. I should like to hear.

ACACIUS. Look, I led quite a worldly life before I entered the convent. I got around, but, I suppose, in some ways I have remained an innocent.

WALBURGA. I have detected an air of innocence about you. It is most becoming.

ACACIUS. *(nervously)* I will confess in my youth there were many men in my life. And I enjoyed my intimacies with them.

WALBURGA. You miss that intimacy, don't you? The world of a celibate is an unnatural one.

ACACIUS. Well, I have found great satisfaction with Jesus. When I first wake up in the morning and every night when I turn out the light, I am joined with him – in prayer.

WALBURGA. Some night the three of us should get together.

ACACIUS. The three of us?

WALBURGA. You, me, and Jesus. Who knows? We might experience an even greater sensation of religious ecstasy.

(AGNES enters with flowers to place on the altar of the Virgin. ACACIUS, very self-conscious, straightens up.)

AGNES. Sisters, am I intruding?

WALBURGA. Not at all. Sister Acacius, I have found our chat most illuminating. Yes, most illuminating.

(She exits.)

ACACIUS. *(tersely)* What are you looking at? Go about your business.

(She exits in WALBURGA's direction. AGNES arranges the flowers on the altar. JEREMY enters.)

JEREMY. Sister? I hope I didn't startle you.

AGNES. Oh, I'm not a Sister. Not yet. I'm merely a postulant.

JEREMY. Well, to be honest, I'm looking for a postulant.

AGNES. You are? Perhaps I can be of help. What is her name?

JEREMY. Agnes.

AGNES. I am Agnes. I can't imagine why anyone should look for me. I've done nothing of merit.

JEREMY. You'd be surprised at how many people are looking for you. It's wonderful to finally make your acquaintance.

(He extends his hand to shake hers and suddenly winces.)

AGNES. You are in pain.

JEREMY. I'm afraid I spend so much time at the typewriter, the fingers on this hand sometimes freeze up. It's not so bad. *(He winces again.)*

AGNES. Let me see.

(She takes his hand and begins to slowly massage it. Inspirational music, perhaps a heavenly choir is heard.)

JEREMY. You have a very gentle touch.

AGNES. Don't say anything.

JEREMY. Your hand is so warm.

AGNES. Shhhhh.

JEREMY. The heat is almost unbearable and yet I don't want to pull away.

*(**SISTER ACACIUS** enters and sees them. **AGNES** lets go of his hand.)*

I can move my thumb. I haven't been able to do that in months.

ACACIUS. Well, what do you know, another miracle is upon us. Agnes, go about your duties.

AGNES. Yes, Sister Acacius.

*(**AGNES** curtsies and exits.)*

ACACIUS. What can I do for you?

JEREMY. I was visiting the school. I hope I haven't accidentally wandered into some place I shouldn't.

ACACIUS. You have. This is the forbidden zone. Men aren't allowed in here. Except for Father Fogarty and he doesn't count as a man.

JEREMY. You look awfully familiar. Have we met before?

ACACIUS. Sir, I shall henceforth ask the questions. How can I help you?

JEREMY. I'm hoping to have an audience with – yes, of course, I know who you are. Lily Wainright. Oh, my God. Lily! It's me. Jeremy. Don't you recognize me?

ACACIUS. *(Her face lights up.)* Jeremy – *(pulls herself back)* Yes, I remember you.

JEREMY. It's been many years. Lil, you became a nun, too?

ACACIUS. I am now Sister Mary Acacius. And that is how you must address me.

JEREMY. I can't believe this. You and Susan both became nuns?

ACACIUS. Yes, we took the same path towards righteousness.

JEREMY. I confess I came here hoping to see Susan, I mean, the Mother Superior. But running into you again is extraordinary. I've missed you, Lil. I mean, Sister Mary Acacius. What a great pal you were. I remember feeling that I could tell you my innermost secrets. Nothing seemed to shock you. Aw, we had swell times.

ACACIUS. What became of you? One day you suddenly disappeared from our lives.

JEREMY. Susan and I had a tremendous fight and like an idiot I took the first overseas assignment I could find. I spent years as a war correspondent. I see now that I was desperately trying to compete with the legend of my father. Big Jack Templeton; the greatest newspaperman of his day. I could never compete with him. I couldn't out drink him. I certainly couldn't out write him. I can tell *you* this but no one else. My father was also famous for the gargantuan size of his penis. Big Jack's notorious twelve inch sinker. Naturally, mine was one inch shorter.

*(**SISTER ACACIUS** desperately tries to maintain her poise, although she is wracked by sexual frustration. Innocent of the effect he has on her, **JEREMY** continues his "confession.")*

JEREMY. Yes, in Tokyo, I paraded my giant schlong in the public bath to intimidate the Japanese men with their small endowments. In Dublin, I hauled out my humongous dick at every urinal so those afflicted with the "Irish inch" could get a good jealous peek. I got my comeuppance when I was seduced into marrying the scandalous American heiress, Valerie Blair. It wasn't till our wedding night when I realized that my bride had purchased me for my celebrated sexual organ. Valerie was obsessed with every facet of my penis; the massive mushroom head and the long shaft that's thicker than a beer can. She liked nothing more than to feel the heavy weight of my low hanging testicles in the palm of her hand. She called them her plump beggar's purses. Gee, thanks for being such a great listener.

(**SISTER ACACIUS** *has melted with sexual desire, but somehow pulls herself together.*)

ACACIUS. Don't mention it.

(**MOTHER SUPERIOR** *enters.*)

MOTHER SUPERIOR. Acacius!

ACACIUS. Reverend Mother, look who I found.

MOTHER SUPERIOR. Jeremy. It's been so long. Sister Acacius, he's hardly changed at all.

ACACIUS. Nooooo.

MOTHER SUPERIOR. Sister, you may leave us. Sister!

JEREMY. Goodbye.

(**ACACIUS** *curtsies and bow-legged with sexual heat exits.*)

Reverend Mother? That's a high muckety muck, isn't it?

MOTHER SUPERIOR. I have many responsibilities.

JEREMY. I always knew that you be the best at anything you chose to do.

MOTHER SUPERIOR. In a religious order, we don't think of ourselves in any way as "best."

JEREMY. From what I hear, you've become an important figure in this community.

MOTHER SUPERIOR. I'm merely spreading God's love. The neighborhood is ever changing. A new clinic just opened around the corner, devoted to women's health and reproductive choices. *(grimly)* We'll see what we can do about that.

JEREMY. *(quickly changing the subject)* Do you still sing? I remember you had a lovely voice.

MOTHER SUPERIOR. Thank you for remembering. I occasionally belt out a few numbers in moments of spiritual reflection.

JEREMY. A pity no one else gets to hear you.

MOTHER SUPERIOR. Ah, you were always trying to lure me into a career in show business.

JEREMY. Perhaps to lure you away from journalism. I didn't appreciate the competition. You were a damn good reporter. Pardon the expression.

MOTHER SUPERIOR. You're forgiven this time.

JEREMY. In your present life, are there opportunities for you to write?

MOTHER SUPERIOR. Oh yes. But I use that gift not to exploit tragic events but to serve God. In fact, I've written a book that is about to be published.

JEREMY. That's wonderful. What sort of book?

MOTHER SUPERIOR. My reaction to a modern world gone astray. What is perceived as a march to freedom, I consider a march towards damnation. I seek a return to the values and morality of an earlier simpler time. My book is titled "The Middle Ages. So Bad?"

JEREMY. You'll be opening yourself up to a storm of controversy.

MOTHER SUPERIOR. Jeremy, you didn't travel all the way to Pittsburgh to discuss my literary efforts.

JEREMY. I'm not sure what I'm looking for. All I know is everything I've accomplished feels meaningless and I find myself plagued by insecurities.

MOTHER SUPERIOR. God is the only answer to man's insecurity.

JEREMY. Perhaps that's why I needed to see you.

MOTHER SUPERIOR. We shall do our best to provide guidance. Jeremy, are you currently working for a newspaper?

JEREMY. No. I gave up journalism a while back. A few years ago, a film company acquired my services by dangling an impressive paycheck in front of me.

MOTHER SUPERIOR. A film company?

JEREMY. I'm engaged in the acquisition and development of new properties.

MOTHER SUPERIOR. I'm sure fascinating stories can be found in the most unlikely of places.

JEREMY. Frequently.

MOTHER SUPERIOR. Even within the walls of a convent. Perhaps a young postulant who sees heavenly visions and has the power to heal could be the premise of a successful motion picture.

JEREMY. It would be a film that could bring inspiration to millions of people around the world.

MOTHER SUPERIOR. And make millions of dollars for your company. Shall we drop all pretense? This nonsense of your search for life's meaning was simply a ruse to talk business with me.

JEREMY. Please, Susan, you mustn't think that I came here merely to –

MOTHER SUPERIOR. I have received numerous requests from your company and ripped them all to shreds. I should have known they would send you as their devil's messenger.

JEREMY. Yes, they sent me here to purchase the rights to Agnes's story but I jumped at the opportunity –

MOTHER SUPERIOR. I have no doubt you did. Jumped high.

JEREMY. I jumped at the opportunity of seeing you again. When I learned that the Mother Superior was the former Susan Appleyard, it seemed like, well, a gift from God.

MOTHER SUPERIOR. How dare you make a mockery of His name? If you so longed to see me, why didn't you seek me out twenty years ago? Why did you abandon me with nary a look back?

JEREMY. I thought a nun renounced all past bitterness.

MOTHER SUPERIOR. We are not perfect creatures.

JEREMY. Then let's forget about the past. It's no secret that your school is in serious trouble. The financial rewards you could reap from this film sale could solve all of your problems.

MOTHER SUPERIOR. I will not exploit that young girl for my own ends.

JEREMY. Perhaps this will be an added inducement. Quite coincidentally, I am a close friend of Mrs. Morris Levinson.

MOTHER SUPERIOR. How do you know Mrs. Levinson?

JEREMY. Her husband was a great friend of my father. In fact, I'm her houseguest while I'm here in Pittsburgh. I consider her a beloved Aunt.

MOTHER SUPERIOR. How touching.

JEREMY. I know you paid her a rather disastrous call yesterday. I believe I could be instrumental in persuading her to make a sizeable donation to St. Veronica's.

MOTHER SUPERIOR. Now you are stooping to blackmail. I really must thank you, Jeremy. You have erased any bittersweet memory of us that may have lingered in my mind. Now please go, and tell your colleagues in Hollywood that the Sisters of St. Veronica's are not for sale. Good day.

(She turns away from him and closes her eyes in prayer. **JEREMY** *realizes there is nothing more to say and exits.)*

(**TIMOTHY**, *a sensitive twelve-year-old student, enters carrying a baseball bat. He interrupts Mother Superior's reverie.*)

TIMOTHY. Reverend Mother? Reverend Mother? Reverend Mother, I'm here for baseball practice.

MOTHER SUPERIOR. Is it that time all ready? Oh, yes, of course, Timothy. And how have we been doing on the baseball diamond?

TIMOTHY. A little better, Reverend Mother. But still nobody wants me on their team.

MOTHER SUPERIOR. Well, we shall soon remedy that.

TIMOTHY. Golly, Reverend Mother, I don't think I'll ever be any good. I'm just rotten.

MOTHER SUPERIOR. I'm surprised at you, Timothy. You're not a quitter. We've only had twenty lessons thus far.

TIMOTHY. Thirty-seven, to be precise.

MOTHER SUPERIOR. Has it been that many? You haven't told Sister Acacius that I've been coaching you. Have you?

TIMOTHY. Gee, Reverend Mother. I'd never do that. Cross my heart and hope to die. I'd never want to get you in trouble.

MOTHER SUPERIOR. It's just that Sister Acacius is in charge of our physical education program and I wouldn't want her to think I was stepping on her tennis shoes, so to speak.

TIMOTHY. Not a soul knows I come here and they never will.

MOTHER SUPERIOR. Well, now, show me how you've been holding the bat.

(**TIMOTHY** *holds the bat in a woeful fashion.*)

MOTHER SUPERIOR. It still doesn't appear to be quite right. For one thing, your legs aren't far enough apart. And sort of sit down in it. Yes, yes, that's much better. Now I'm no Mickey Mantle or Roger Maris, but I believe the bat should be held almost parallel to your shoulder.

Yes, that's right, Timothy. You're getting it and just keep your eye focused on that ball.

TIMOTHY. Like your eyes are on Jesus?

MOTHER SUPERIOR. Exactly. You're a good boy. Now swing!

(He tries to swing the bat and then despairs.)

TIMOTHY. Oh, what's the use, Reverend Mother. I'll never be good enough. I can't even tell you the name everyone calls me.

MOTHER SUPERIOR. Timothy, what do they call you? Childhood names can be painful but in retrospect never all that bad.

TIMOTHY. A cock-sucking faggot.

MOTHER SUPERIOR. What does Sister Acacius say when they call you that?

TIMOTHY. She's the one who started it.

MOTHER SUPERIOR. Well, she just doesn't want the other boys to think she's playing favorites. Here, let's try again. This time I'm going to pretend I'm pitching. Here we go. Ready?

(MOTHER SUPERIOR *mimes winding up and pitching the ball, but* **TIMOTHY** *gives up and starts to cry. He moves away from her and covers his eyes.)*

Timothy, now what's the matter?

(She goes over and comforts him.)

TIMOTHY. Golly, I'm sorry, Reverend Mother. I guess I am acting like a little fairy.

MOTHER SUPERIOR. Is there something else that's bothering you?

TIMOTHY. It's hard for me to talk about.

MOTHER SUPERIOR. Why don't you try? Perhaps I can be of some help.

TIMOTHY. You can be enormously sympathetic. Reverend Mother, have you ever really liked someone, liked them so much it hurt and wanted them to be your friend but you don't know how to let 'em know you want to be their friend?

MOTHER SUPERIOR. And who do you want to be friends with?

TIMOTHY. Kevin Shaughnessy.

MOTHER SUPERIOR. Kevin Shaughnessy. He's our star athlete. But wasn't he the one who was bullying you the worst?

TIMOTHY. Yeah, but he's not so bad anymore. I think he's a great guy.

MOTHER SUPERIOR. What is it you like about him? Sometimes what we admire in others are simply the qualities we wish to possess in ourselves.

TIMOTHY. Well, I know it's kind of silly but I like hearing the funny way he talks while he's eating. And I like watching him race across the courtyard when he's late for class. I like the pretty way his hair falls across his forehead. And how he smells when he finishes wrestling practice. And seeing the sweat catch above his upper lip. I like his hairy armpits. And I –

MOTHER SUPERIOR. A'hem, yes, he's an admirable sort of fellow.

TIMOTHY. Should I just come out and tell Kevin how much I like him? What if he hauls off and belts me? He might just tackle me and pin me to the ground. Well, I guess I could handle that.

MOTHER SUPERIOR. Timothy, sometimes it's best not to say anything.

TIMOTHY. Keep a secret? But that's like telling a lie and I thought lying was a sin.

MOTHER SUPERIOR. It's just that some personal feelings are better kept to oneself. You might want to try placing them in a beautiful imaginary box.

TIMOTHY. A jewelry box?

MOTHER SUPERIOR. How about a cigar box?

TIMOTHY. I'd rather it be a jewelry box, covered with rhinestones and lined in red velvet?

MOTHER SUPERIOR. Yes, well, I think you should try putting all those special feelings into that box and lock it shut with a large silver key. Then bury the box in a secret imaginary hiding place. In time, you'll forget where you buried it and in time, you'll forget you ever had those feelings.

(An old Scottish charwoman, MRS. MACDUFFIE, enters with her mop and bucket.)

MRS. MACDUFFIE. Mother Superior, if you don't mind, I'd like to scrub this courtyard.

MOTHER SUPERIOR. But of course, Mrs. MacDuffie. Timothy, I think we've done enough for today.

TIMOTHY. Sure thing, Reverend Mother. Thanks for everything.

(TIMOTHY exits. MRS. MACDUFFIE bends over and winces with back pain.)

MOTHER SUPERIOR. Mrs. MacDuffie, are you all right?

MRS. MACDUFFIE. Just this bad back. Too many years scrubbing floors I guess.

MOTHER SUPERIOR. You've been at St. Veronica's a long time. Longer than even myself.

MRS. MACDUFFIE. I know every stone in this building like I know the liver spots on my face.

MOTHER SUPERIOR. Did you come here as a young girl?

MRS. MACDUFFIE. Oh no. I was already a widow woman. Before that I was a maid in the home of Mrs. Levinson. You know her? Mrs. Morris Levinson?

MOTHER SUPERIOR. Indeed I do. In fact, I should like to know her better.

MRS. MACDUFFIE. If you're looking for money, it's a waste of time squeezing a buck out of that old Hebe.

MOTHER SUPERIOR. I won't have you call Mrs. Levinson old.

MRS. MACDUFFIE. As far as I'm concerned, she's a penny pinching tightwad with the morals of a cat in heat.

MOTHER SUPERIOR. I'm afraid I must put an end to this conversation.

MRS. MACDUFFIE. Humph. She poses as a grieving widow but I knows for a fact that she cheated on her husband as soon as she knew he was dead.

MOTHER SUPERIOR. There is no sin in that.

MRS. MACDUFFIE. I'm talking about the first time he died.

MOTHER SUPERIOR. I beg your pardon.

MRS. MACDUFFIE. I was working for her when Mr. Levinson was in that plane crash.

MOTHER SUPERIOR. Over the Congo sometime in the twenties, wasn't it?

MRS. MACDUFFIE. 1926. Yes, Ma'am. It sure looked like he was killed in that crash but no body was found. As soon as she thought he was dead, she indulged in a dirty affair with the gardener. Abatelli.

MOTHER SUPERIOR. Really, Mrs. MacDuffie.

MRS. MACDUFFIE. One day, she learns Mr. Levinson is still alive. So, she runs off to San Francisco for six months.

MOTHER SUPERIOR. I see nothing out of the ordinary in this story.

MRS. MACDUFFIE. Reverend Mother, she done got herself pregnant from the gardener and went to San Francisco to have the baby where no one knew her.

MOTHER SUPERIOR. This is merely conjecture.

MRS. MACDUFFIE. This ain't merely confec -convec – Think I'm making this up, eh? Well, there's more. After she comes back slim and stylish as can be, I find myself dusting that room she calls the library. I just happened to take a hairpin and opened up a drawer in her desk and what do I find but a stack of papers, all from an orphanage in San Francisco. Yes, Ma'am, I remember it as if it were yesterday, even though it be forty years. It was the Carothers Foundling Home. 226 Powell. I even remember the date of the baby's birth. August 23rd, 1926. Hair; red, eyes; green, six pounds, two ounces. That's why I was fired. I knew too much.

(**MRS. MACDUFFE** *exits.* **MOTHER SUPERIOR** *is*
haunted and disturbed by this revelation.)

MOTHER SUPERIOR. August 23rd, 1926.

End of Scene

Scene Six

*(The convent courtyard. **AGNES** is near the statue of the Virgin munching on something green. **SISTER ACACIUS** enters.)*

ACACIUS. Agnes, you nitwit, what in heaven's name are you munching on?

AGNES. My voices have told me to eat the flowers of the earth.

ACACIUS. Not my prized geraniums. What else have your voices told you to do? Take a crap in the Confessional?

AGNES. St. Clare has told me that I – it was hard to understand. She said – She told me that I was the Immaculate Conception.

ACACIUS. What did you say?

AGNES. I didn't say it. She said it. I am the Immaculate Conception.

ACACIUS. That does it. That does it. That proves you're a fake. No one can *be* the Immaculate Conception. The creation of the Virgin Mary's soul *was* the Immaculate Conception. You don't know what the hell you're blabbering about.

AGNES. That's what she said! I am the immaculate conception. *(with a glint of madness in her eyes)* I AM THE IMMACULATE CONCEPTION!

ACACIUS. Believe it or not, kid, I worry for you. This craziness of yours can only lead to disaster.

AGNES. If that is so, then disaster be my destiny.

ACACIUS. Oh, boy. Oh boy, have I got the goods on you.

AGNES. You do?

ACACIUS. Oh, yeah. I know your kind. You crave being the center of attention, don't you? The great star! Well, there's no room in a convent for that sort of EGOMANIA!

AGNES. I've told you the truth. You just don't believe. You've got to have faith.

ACACIUS. It's nearly time for chapel. Get yourself cleaned up. You look horrible and you smell like dung.

AGNES. Yes, Sister Acacius.

(She curtsies and exits. ACACIUS *crosses to the statue and prays.)*

ACACIUS. Blessed Mother, why am I so cruel to this child? God forgive me. I have persecuted her because I am wracked with guilt. I hold a secret about her that I must carry to my grave. And now fate has brought her to this convent where I see her embracing the simple pure faith I have lost. Without that faith, my body is a well of emptiness. An enormous cavity that must be filled. I can no longer go on like this. I must confess my sins. I must confess.

*(*MOTHER SUPERIOR *enters.)*

MOTHER SUPERIOR. Acacius, were you speaking to me?

ACACIUS. *(desperately)* No – , but yes, I must speak to you.

MOTHER SUPERIOR. Is this an urgent matter?

ACACIUS. Most urgent. It's about the postulant Agnes.

MOTHER SUPERIOR. What has she done now? I'm really in a dreadful hurry.

ACACIUS. I beg of you. Please, take a moment.

MOTHER SUPERIOR. I'm afraid I can't. I've just received startling news. I must see Mrs. Levinson immediately. I understand she is leaving the country first thing tomorrow morning.

ACACIUS. But please, you must listen to me. There is an ugly truth that I live with, that I cannot bear any longer. You must absolve me of my guilt.

MOTHER SUPERIOR. All right. All right. Let us calm down. My dear, what is it – you can't face? *(Her affected accent makes it sound like she said, "What is it, you cunt face?")*

ACACIUS. What did you say?

MOTHER SUPERIOR. I really don't have the time for this. I said, "What is it you can't face?"

ACACIUS. You called me "cunt face?"

MOTHER SUPERIOR. That is not what I said.

ACACIUS. That is what you said. You called me "cunt face."
You called me "cunt face." I come to you pleading for
council and you call me "cunt face." There are some
things that are unforgivable.

MOTHER SUPERIOR. Oh, but –

ACACIUS. Unforgivable!

(She storms off. **MOTHER SUPERIOR** *calls after her.)*

MOTHER SUPERIOR. Acacius! Lil!

(In a dreadful hurry, **MOTHER SUPERIOR** *exits in the
opposite direction.)*

End of Scene

Scene Seven

(MRS. LEVINSON's drawing room. MOTHER SUPERIOR *confronts her.*

MRS. LEVINSON. After our last meeting, I was of the firm belief that there was nothing more to be said between us.

MOTHER SUPERIOR. Mrs. Levinson, alas, there is much to be said.

MRS. LEVINSON. If you are expecting me to acquiesce to your demands for money or my house, you shall be cruelly disappointed.

MOTHER SUPERIOR. It seems that an old charwoman at our school was many years ago in your employ as a maid. At that time, she came across papers detailing an infant's admission to a San Francisco orphanage. The baby's date of birth was August 23, 1926. That is the day I was born and I was raised in that very same institution.

MRS. LEVINSON. A genuine coincidence I will admit.

MOTHER SUPERIOR. The greater coincidence is that our paths should cross once more. I am fully convinced that you are my mother and that you abandoned me when I became an inconvenience.

MRS. LEVINSON. I will not be spoken to in this manner. Please, leave at once or I shall have you removed.

MOTHER SUPERIOR. Erasing me from your life this time will not be as simple. That selfish act condemned me to a loveless childhood in a brutal, sadistic institution. Oh, I could level you with guilt if I told you all that I suffered at the hands of Mr. and Mrs. Carothers, the couple who ran the orphanage, but I won't. Such revenge is contrary to my faith. Oh, I could give you eternal nightmares if I revealed how the drunken Mr. Carothers would dress up as a red devil with horns and a pitchfork and use me as his child whore in the most perverse of sexual bacchanalia. But I won't. That would be too easy. Oh, I could tell you things about the Carothers' degenerate erotic calisthenics involving a bicycle pump, rubber cement and Purina's Cream of Wheat. But I won't. By any account, I should have gone mad. Perhaps I was mad. But through it all, I clung to the fantasy that my mother lived, that she was somewhere in the world, caring and affectionate, regretting her fatal decision and wanting me returned to her loving arms.

MRS. LEVINSON. Bravo, my dear, bravo. You are a clever little actress. Your eyes are moistened with tears. Your voice trembles with emotion, but I am not moved. Over the years, I have encountered numerous pretenders for the role of my long lost daughter. Eventually, all were exposed as imposters. I should have thought your devout beliefs would have kept you from this vulgar impersonation. But I see the Levinson fortune was too much for even you to ignore.

MOTHER SUPERIOR. You can never know what it's like to forever think of yourself as an unwanted orphan. There is always the sense of something missing. An essential puzzle piece lost. You can try to replace it with other things, other beliefs, but nothing will ever fit.

MRS. LEVINSON. How unfortunate for you, but that is not my affair. Now I must request you take your leave.

MOTHER SUPERIOR. You are hard. Why did I come here? I don't know. I suppose I longed to hear some words of regret. Or experience a brief moment of maternal tenderness. But I see that you are incapable of those human feelings.

MRS. LEVINSON. Get out of my house. Leave me alone.

MOTHER SUPERIOR. My barbs are striking home. I can take some satisfaction in that.

MRS. LEVINSON. I am far from tears.

MOTHER SUPERIOR. Goodbye, Mrs. Levinson.

(She turns to leave.)

MRS. LEVINSON. You confuse me. I'm an old woman. I'm leaving tomorrow on a cruise to the Encantadas, but in a few weeks, upon my return, visit me again and perhaps then cooler heads shall prevail.

MOTHER SUPERIOR. No, I shall never come back. The mother in my dreams does not live in this house. This is the house of the dead. *(She begins to gag.)* Please, excuse me. *(She gags again.)*

MRS. LEVINSON. My dear, are you ill?

MOTHER SUPERIOR. I'm fine. I gag whenever I become emotional. *(She gags again.)*

MRS. LEVINSON. *(tremulously)* Oh my. Oh my, I also gag when I become overwrought. *(She begins to gag.)* And so did my mother. And my grandmother. And my cousin Yetta. *(gags again)* My darling, I can fight the truth no longer. I am your mother!

(The two women embrace and both gag. **MOTHER SUPERIOR** *sobs and* **MRS. LEVINSON** *holds her in her arms.)*

MRS. LEVINSON. My darling. My darling. Let us both weep for time wasted. I'm so sorry. I am so sorry.

MOTHER SUPERIOR. Mother –

MRS. LEVINSON. You spoke of something missing. I too have lived with that loss. Love. That is what has been missing. This beautiful house should have been a happy one. Yes, it is a dead thing. A mausoleum. Together, we could bring it back to life.

MOTHER SUPERIOR. Please. Please.

MRS. LEVINSON. Can you possibly forgive a foolish old woman? The past cannot be undone but do let me try and make it up to you. Give me that chance.

MOTHER SUPERIOR. Oh, Mother.

(They both begin to gag.)

End of Scene

Scene Eight

(The catacomb. **BROTHER VENERIUS** *has arrived first.*
SISTER WALBURGA *enters.)*

VENERIUS. You are late.

WALBURGA. I could not get away without being seen.

VENERIUS. We have been exceedingly patient with you.
When will you have done the deed?

WALBURGA. It will be done.

VENERIUS. But when?

WALBURGA. You do not give me orders.

VENERIUS. I shall give you orders. I am an emissary for the
Church of the Divine Sister.

WALBURGA. You will get off my back! The time must be perfect.

VENERIUS. Time is running out.

WALBURGA. I am the expert in such matters. You take your
orders from me.

VENERIUS. I take my orders from the suppressed and forbidden gospel of St. Gladys; the gospel that tells us of
the true bedrock of the Christian faith; a gospel that
will one day fill the emptiness of the void that is our
modern Godless world.

WALBURGA. You do not need to instruct me on the prin-
ciples of our religion.

VENERIUS. Perhaps I do. Perhaps further instruction will
inspire you to do your job; a job you for which you are
being highly paid from our Church coffers.

WALBURGA. Do you not think I fling myself on the cold
stone floor every morning in humiliation to our
Savior? The daughter of God. The older sister of Jesus
Christ, the divine Joyce.

VENERIUS. How foolish are those who insist that the brother of Joyce was the Messiah. Jesus loved his sister with a devotion he felt for no one besides his Virgin mother. However, it was Joyce who performed the miracles. It was Joyce who gave the Sermon on the Mount. Jesus would have been the first to have given her credit but the disciples felt a woman would not be accepted as the leader of a great religion.

WALBURGA. If you so revere the womanhood of our Messiah, perhaps you could give me the respect I deserve.

VENERIUS. You will have my undying respect once you perform the deed for which you were sent for.

WALBURGA. It will be done and the world will tremble.

End of Scene

Scene Nine

(The convent courtyard. **MOTHER SUPERIOR** *enters with* **MRS. LEVINSON**. *Mrs. Levinson seems like a completely different person, outgoing and full of love.)*

MOTHER SUPERIOR. So you see, Mother, that the children really do deserve something better.

MRS. LEVINSON. How right you are. How could I have been so selfish? First things first, we move the school into my home until the Levinson Foundation can build you a beautiful brand new facility. I'll take the small maid's room above the garage. How thrilling it will be to hear children's laughter ringing through the house.

MOTHER SUPERIOR. I love you.

MRS. LEVINSON. And I love you, my precious child.

MOTHER SUPERIOR. But I love you more, Mummy.

MRS. LEVINSON. No, no, no, I love you more, Gum drop.

*(***MOTHER SUPERIOR*** imitates a baby gurgling.)*

So, Daughter, what's next on our grand tour?

MOTHER SUPERIOR. I think I've introduced you to all the Sisters. But where is Sister Acacius? She's been acting so strange lately.

*(***SISTER WALBURGA*** enters with ***SISTER ACACIUS***. ***ACACIUS*** acts strangely remote and taciturn.)*

WALBURGA. Here she is. Here is the missing person.

MOTHER SUPERIOR. Acacius, you look pale.

ACACIUS. Do I?

MOTHER SUPERIOR. So much has happened. I know you've met before but I want to introduce you again, this time to my mother.

MRS. LEVINSON. Please forgive my dreadful rudeness during our last encounter.

ACACIUS. Only *He* can forgive and that in the next world.

MOTHER SUPERIOR. Well, get this. Mom is going to loan us her house until her foundation can build us a new school. And to raise public awareness, next Saturday we going to hold an enormous charity bazaar.

MRS. LEVINSON. It's all so exciting. We have a great many plans.

MOTHER SUPERIOR. It is exciting. We can have a science competition, an art show, a bake sale, and a crafts fair. Sister Joseph will make her delicious caramels and Brother Leonard his lavender sachets. Acacius, you can organize a wrestling tournament. To top it off, we should have some sort of marvelous religious pageant. Walburga, perhaps you could direct.

WALBURGA. Me? Direct?

MOTHER SUPERIOR. I understand years ago you worked with a comedy improv group in Nuremberg. My only request, Sister Walburga, is that you devise something very special for the triplets.

MRS. LEVINSON. The triplets?

MOTHER SUPERIOR. Marilyn, Carolyn, and Harolyn. Three adorable young ladies, sophomores.

ACACIUS. Reverend Mother's private goon squad. Her secret police.

MOTHER SUPERIOR. None of that, Acacius. Those darling girls were cleared of all suspicion of water torture.

MRS. LEVINSON. Sister Maria Walburga, have you remained in touch with any of your former theatrical colleagues?

WALBURGA. Nein. I have always been something of a loner. But there was one girl with whom I was intimate. Her name was Herta Feinshmecker. A lovely girl. During the war she worked for the Gestapo, but was in fact a quadruple agent. Her loyalties were so complex that after the war she held the distinction of being the only cabaret performer to be condemned on the floor of the United Nations. From that point onward she was banned from the comedy circuit. Vilified, blacklisted. Paraded nude through the streets of Heidelberg, while the band played oom pah pah, oom pah pah. After years of torment, she was at last embraced by a church sect whose radical beliefs ran contrary to those of his Holiness in Rome. They trained her as an international Catholic hit woman with the code name, Domino. But through all this she never lost her sense of humor.

MRS. LEVINSON. And have you remained friends?

WALBURGA. Nein. We are no longer buddies. It has been painful. We were as if one person; possessed of one mind, one heart, one vulva.

MOTHER SUPERIOR. Well, I think you're better off without her. Acacius, what is that poking out of your habit?

ACACIUS. A hanky.

(**MOTHER SUPERIOR** *tugs at a flashy piece of fabric sticking out of* **ACACIUS**' *habit and pulls it out. It's a trashy looking cocktail dress.*)

MOTHER SUPERIOR. What is this?

ACACIUS. What do you think it is? It's a cocktail dress. I confiscated it from one of the girls' rooms. I was on my way to toss this vile piece of devil's rubbish into the trash. You think I wanted it for myself? You think "Old Cunt Face" wants to put it on and parade in front of the mirror with her knockers hanging out? Is that what you're thinking, Mother Superior?

MOTHER SUPERIOR. *(trying to calm her down)* Not at all. Of course you found it in one of the girls' rooms. And now, I shall put this dress in the charity bin.

(**ACACIUS** *violently grabs it back from her.*)

ACACIUS. I shall do it, Reverend Mother. No need for you to sully your hands with this filth.

MRS. LEVINSON. I imagine young girls can be a handful. I wish I hadn't missed out on that opportunity with my own daughter.

MOTHER SUPERIOR. We have many years left.

WALBURGA. Fewer than you may think?

MOTHER SUPERIOR. I beg your pardon?

WALBURGA. Our time on earth is short. It is only in Heaven that we find eternal happiness.

MOTHER SUPERIOR. Okay. We should get going. Mom, want to see my room?

(They exit.)

WALBURGA. Sister Acacius, you seem distracted.

ACACIUS. I'm perfectly fine.

WALBURGA. I can almost hear your heart beating.

ACACIUS. No, it's not.

WALBURGA. What's bugging you, Acacius? Do you need a haircut? I brought my clippers with me from Berlin. It has a triple zero attachment.

ACACIUS. No, no, I'm all right. I had a buzz cut last week.

WALBURGA. You have been acting very peculiar. I shall be watching you.

*(***WALBURGA*** exits with an air of suspicion.)*

ACACIUS. My Lord, strike me down for what I've done. Give me hives. Give me boils. Give me eternal chafing. Is there no way to rectify my evil? Yes, Yes. I shall write to Jeremy. He can absolve me of my guilt. I shall write him immediately.

End of Scene

Scene Ten

(Mrs. Levinson's home. **JEREMY** *reads the letter aloud to* **MRS. LEVINSON**.

JEREMY. *(reading)* Dear Jeremy, I write this letter to you not as Sister Acacius but as my true self, Lillian Doris Wainright. Old friend, I have done you an unforgivable injustice. You and my beloved Susan. Years ago, when you disappeared from our lives, Susan discovered she was pregnant with your child. *(to* **MRS. LEVINSON**, *emotionally)* I can't believe this. I'm almost afraid to read on. I'm not sure I can.

MRS. LEVINSON. If you find it too painful, perhaps it would help if you read the letter in the voice of Sister Acacius.

JEREMY. I'll try. *(He reads in the New York accent of* **SISTER ACACIUS**.*)* Jeremy, what can I tell you, fate seemed to turn against us. We lost our jobs and were nearly starving. In this atmosphere of despair, your child was born. A girl. *(Overcome, he puts the letter down.)* I can't read anymore.

MRS. LEVINSON. Here, let me. *(She picks up the letter and continues reading aloud, also in the voice of* **SISTER ACACIUS**.*)* Susan became deathly ill immediately after giving birth and fell into a coma. I panicked and thinking I was doing right for everyone, took the baby to Pittsburgh and gave the child up for adoption. *(She too is overcome and puts down the letter.)* My heart. I can't take anymore. You'll have to finish reading it.

*(***JEREMY** *takes the letter from her and continues reading aloud in the voice of* **SISTER ACACIUS**.*)*

JEREMY. When Susan came out of her coma, I told her the baby had died. Only God can forgive me. Sincerely yours, Lil AKA Sister Acacius.

MRS. LEVINSON. Why? Why must this horrendous history repeat itself? I've found my daughter only to lose my granddaughter.

JEREMY. That dingbat stole my baby.

End of Scene

Scene Eleven

(The convent. **SISTER ACACIUS** *has gone mad.)*

ACACIUS. I have confessed my sins but my admission of guilt renders me no peace. Dark clouds loom above. And the birds. Are those black crows circling me? Is it because I am also a black crow? Pecking. Pecking. Pecking. I must be a beautiful bird. A robin red breast. A cockatoo. I must remove these black robes.

(She begins stripping off her habit.)

I can't breathe in these heavy vestments. The very threads are a spider's web. They must be burned. Burned to cinders.

(She has stripped off her habit and is wearing a white union suit. Her hair is cropped short. She puts the flashy cocktail dress on over her union suit.)

It's been so long since I've worn a pretty dress. A girl can't go out on the town without her lipstick. Where is it? Where did I hide it?

(She takes out of her décolletage a bright red lipstick and without using a mirror, draws a grotesque line all around her mouth. She looks like a demented clown. **JEREMY** *enters.)*

JEREMY. Oh, my God.

ACACIUS. Yes, it's me. Lily.

JEREMY. What's happened to you?

ACACIUS. Not sure this dress is doing much for me. Is it the color?

JEREMY. What happened to the baby? Do you know where she is today?

ACACIUS. The baby? What baby?

JEREMY. My daughter! What happened to my child?

ACACIUS. You want a child? I could give you babies. I'm surprisingly fertile. Jeremy, take me away from this dark place. I'll go anywhere you want. Only quickly. They'll be back.

(She rubs her body close to his. **MOTHER SUPERIOR** *enters.)*

MOTHER SUPERIOR. Acacius!

JEREMY. She's gone mad.

*(***MOTHER SUPERIOR*** *grabs* **ACACIUS** *and shakes her.)*

MOTHER SUPERIOR. Stop this, Lily. Stop this at once! Do you hear me? Stop it!

(Suddenly, **ACACIUS** *comes to her senses. She wakes as if almost from a dream. She begins to sob in* **MOTHER SUPERIOR***'s arms.)*

ACACIUS. Dear God. Dear God.

MOTHER SUPERIOR. Shhhhh. Don't talk.

ACACIUS. I took the baby. She didn't die. She lives.

MOTHER SUPERIOR. The baby? What are you saying?

JEREMY. Our baby. She thought she was helping you. When you were in the coma after the child's birth, Lily gave the baby to an adoption agency. Later, she told you the baby had died.

MOTHER SUPERIOR. I refuse to believe any of this.

ACACIUS. It's true. All of it is true. But there's more. I took the baby on the Greyhound from New York to Pittsburgh. Somewhere far enough that I would never be tempted to see her again. Imagine my horror when you and I were transferred to St. Veronica's in this very same city.

MOTHER SUPERIOR. She's here in Pittsburgh?

ACACIUS. It gets worse. She's not only in Pittsburgh but in this convent. It was God's will that the child joined our order as a postulant. She calls herself Agnes.

*(***AGNES*** *enters unbeknownst to them. She listens to what they're saying.)*

MOTHER SUPERIOR. Agnes is my daughter?

JEREMY. Our daughter?

ACACIUS. Yes, Agnes is your child that I gave away twenty years ago.

MOTHER SUPERIOR. How long have you known this?

ACACIUS. I figured it out the moment she arrived. Agnes is indeed the bastard fruit of your womb.

AGNES. NOOOOOOOO!!!! It's not TRUE!

MOTHER SUPERIOR. Yes, my dear. It is true. I am your mother.

AGNES. That cannot be so. I am the Immaculate Conception.

ACACIUS. Here she goes.

JEREMY. And I am your father.

AGNES. Then my voices have lied! They have tricked me! It was all a lie! No! No! No!

(She runs off hysterically sobbing.)

MOTHER SUPERIOR. What have we done? What have we done?

JEREMY. Such a brutal way of finding out the truth.

MOTHER SUPERIOR. Jeremy, I'm worried.

ACACIUS. Let me speak to the child. I'll be the voice of sanity.

(ACACIUS picks up her discarded habit and exits.)

JEREMY. Well, this changes everything.

MOTHER SUPERIOR. How so?

JEREMY. Suddenly we're a family. We have a child who needs us. And Susan, I need you.

MOTHER SUPERIOR. Jeremy, please.

JEREMY. I love you, Susan. I've always loved you. And I know you love me. Does the Bible not say that the greatest love of all is between a man and a woman and anything else is an abomination?

MOTHER SUPERIOR. Such a beautiful sentiment.

(He takes her in his arms.)

JEREMY. Come away with me, darling. Let our past become our future. Come away with me tonight.

MOTHER SUPERIOR. Tonight? Would that it were possible.

JEREMY. I can't bear one more minute without you.

MOTHER SUPERIOR. Jeremy, please.

(She pulls away.)

Jeremy, how I've missed you. Your strength, your sense of play. Indeed, for a moment I nearly betrayed one whose all consuming love has meant more to me than breath itself.

JEREMY. But Jesus is not a real man. He's a concept, a myth.

MOTHER SUPERIOR. Oh, he's very real. As substantial as the stone walls of Jerusalem. Jeremy, we can't go back in time. But we can still love each other. But only you can make that possible.

JEREMY. Tell me how. Give me instruction. I'd do anything rather than lose you.

MOTHER SUPERIOR. By joining me in a strict vow of chastity. But in denying any physical expression of our love, we could enjoy a form of passion that could not be censured.

JEREMY. *(dubious)* Really?

MOTHER SUPERIOR. You would become in effect a sacred eunuch. And there are pills that can help you achieve that goal. I am told, in some cases, over time, men have found their penis to become radically shortened and their testicles shrunk to the size of little pine nuts.

JEREMY. Well...It's certainly something to think about.

MOTHER SUPERIOR. Don't wait too long. God's love is eternal, but even he works on a deadline. However, we do have an urgent matter to discuss. Come, there is a room upstairs where we can talk.

(They exit.)

End of Scene

Scene Twelve

*(The charity bazaar. A string of colored lights is draped across the stage. Sound effects of children laughing and music playing and carnival rides. **ACACIUS** enters and goes into the audience and speaks to them.)*

ACACIUS. Sister Michael, raise these lights a bit higher. We don't want the children to get electrocuted. Sister Claude, don't you dare drop those cupcakes. Parkinson's is no excuse. Hey, hey, hey, Marvel Ann, don't you try and fool me. I see smoke emitting from between your lips. Spit out that Lucky Strike right now. Kathleen O'Connor, God doesn't like that wiggle in your walk, and neither do I. Lydia and Patrick, keep your hands to yourselves. Everyone, have fun. Enjoy the bazaar.

*(She exits, just as **MOTHER SUPERIOR** enters with **MRS. LEVINSON**.)*

MOTHER SUPERIOR. Mother, we must get you some funnel cake. Sister Felicity's specialty. Sister F! We have another hungry mouth for you.

MRS. LEVINSON. No, no, please. My dear, you are stuffing me like a prized goose. There are simply too many wonderful things to eat and to see.

MOTHER SUPERIOR. The bazaar is a grand success, isn't it?

MRS. LEVINSON. I am so very proud of you. But I must say, I found some of the activities a tad disturbing.

MOTHER SUPERIOR. Oh, you mean Marilyn, Carolyn and Harolyn?

MRS. LEVINSON. I never knew a potato sack race could turn so...ugly.

MOTHER SUPERIOR. The triplets play to win. Have you seen Agnes? She's having lunch with Jeremy.

MRS. LEVINSON. Has she calmed down a bit?

MOTHER SUPERIOR. For some reason, she finds accepting Jeremy as her father easier than me as her mother.

(SISTER WALBURGA enters carrying a clipboard.)

WALBURGA. Reverend Mother? We are experiencing some difficulties with the girls' leather corsets.

MOTHER SUPERIOR. Sister Walburga has taken complete charge of the pageant. She hasn't allowed me to attend even a single rehearsal.

WALBURGA. I am something of a perfectionist.

MRS. LEVINSON. I'm sure it will be stupendous and perfectly divine.

WALBURGA. It will have a beginning, a middle and most definitely an end.

(WALBURGA exits.)

MRS. LEVINSON. Strange creature.

MOTHER SUPERIOR. Stranger by the minute. The other day I found a telegram evidently sent here over a week ago. One of the elderly sisters must have misplaced it. It was from the Mother House in Berlin, informing me that Sister Maria Walburga would not be joining our order as planned. She was sent instead to teach the accordion in a leper colony in Tunisia.

MRS. LEVINSON. So then, who is this person who claims to be Sister Walburga?

MOTHER SUPERIOR. Well, we mustn't jump to any conclusions. But I must say, it fills me with doubt. Yes, doubt.

(JEREMY enters with AGNES, who is wearing a very tight, short dress, spike heels, and a huge 1960's teased hairdo. She's carrying her small suitcase and acts tough as nails.)

JEREMY. Hope we're not late. Have we missed very much?

MOTHER SUPERIOR. It's been a lovely day with more to come.

MRS. LEVINSON. Agnes, what an interesting outfit.

MOTHER SUPERIOR. By that provocative get-up, am I to assume you will be leaving St. Veronica's?

AGNES. Quick on the draw, Mother. Yeah, I'd say you could safely assume that. I can't wait to haul my ass out of this shithole.

(ACACIUS enters and gasps when she sees AGNES' wild outfit.)

ACACIUS. Agnes! Look at you!

AGNES. Yeah, what is it, Cunt Face?

ACACIUS. Did she just call me Cunt Face?

MOTHER SUPERIOR. No, no. You just misunderstood her.

ACACIUS. She's leaving the convent?

AGNES. You got it right, Butch. I'm heading westward to Vegas.

MRS. LEVINSON. Why on earth Las Vegas? That's no place for a sensitive young girl.

JEREMY. She wants a career in show business. I have contacts at some of the larger casinos.

MOTHER SUPERIOR. Agnes, I imagine you think I'll disapprove of such a career. But in my deepest heart, I wish you every happiness.

AGNES. Go fuck yourself with a cucumber.

MRS. LEVINSON. You mustn't speak to your mother that way.

AGNES. I was happier as an orphan. Now I have a mother but God is dead.

MRS. LEVINSON. Now, darling, Atheism isn't such a bad thing. Sweetie, I'm going to run to my car and grab some brochures from my Atheist groups. We have all sorts of wholesome, fun activities for young non-believers. I'll be back before you can say, "Heaven is Outer Space and Hell is outta sight." *(She runs off.)*

MOTHER SUPERIOR. Agnes, there are many successful performers who maintain a rigorous spiritual life. Jeremy, do you think you could use your influence and book me to sing on a few well-chosen television shows? Mike Douglas or Merv Griffin? What a splendid way to promote my book and bring millions of people closer to God.

JEREMY. I think I could do that.

(**SISTER WALBURGA** *enters and listens intently to* **MOTHER SUPERIOR.**)

MOTHER SUPERIOR. Of course, all the proceeds from my book will go directly into the fund to tear down the old St. Veronica's and build the new one.

ACACIUS. I sure will miss the old girl. Perhaps you're being too hasty.

JEREMY. Must it really come down? I think it's a tragic mistake.

AGNES. I want to see it fucking explode and with all the nuns inside.

MOTHER SUPERIOR. Now listen all of you characters and listen good. Everyone here seems to have some sort of ax to grind. As the children say nowadays, cool it. We are graced today with the presence of a number of important city and state officials. We will need all of their enthusiasm to facilitate the immediate demolition of St. Veronica's.

(**SISTER WALBURGA** *shocks them all by whipping a gun out of her habit.*)

WALBURGA. Nobody move!

JEREMY. Okay. Let's not get excited.

MOTHER SUPERIOR. Walburga, what on earth are you doing with that gun? There are children nearby.

WALBURGA. Allow me to make myself more comfortable.

(She begins removing pieces of her habit.)

ACACIUS. Walburga, you grew your hair out!

WALBURGA. Shut up, Cunt Face.

ACACIUS. Now, I know I heard that right.

WALBURGA. I suppose it is only fair that I reveal my true identity. I was not sent here from the Mother house in Berlin. I am on assignment from the Order of the Divine Sister. I am Herta Feinshmecker. Code name: Domino. This building will not be torn down.

(She removes the rest of her habit and is garbed in a tight fitting black leather jumpsuit.)

MOTHER SUPERIOR. My dear, Fraulein Feinshmecker, I'm touched by your affection for St. Veronica's but really, despite its age, the architecture is not terribly distinguished.

WALBURGA. I do not give a tinker's damn about the building but what lies beneath. A sarcophagus which must not be disturbed. In it lies the miraculously preserved body of the elder sister of Jesus and the true Messiah; the divine Joyce.

JEREMY. Joyce Christ. Never heard of her.

WALBURGA. Her glory has been suppressed lo these many centuries by corrupt male clerics; her remains hidden on the coast of Spain. Just as the Pope's infidels were about to have her body desecrated, she was rescued by the great High Priestess, Norma Columbus. In dark of night, she had the body removed to the hold of the ship "The Pinta" which her brother was sailing to the New World. Christopher Columbus delivered Joyce to the Iroquois Indians who buried her here in Pittsburgh.

AGNES. How can any corpse be preserved for two thousand years?

WALBURGA. Funny you should ask. I took a peek at her last night. I tell you, we should all look so good. Rauschmitten! Schnell! We of the faith believe with all our hearts that someday soon Joyce will be resurrected. She will rise.

JEREMY. What a story. What a picture this would make.

WALBURGA. Don't come any closer.

MOTHER SUPERIOR. My dear, let's be sensible. I am truly fascinated to learn that I have a sister-in-law, Joyce, residing in the cellar. But relatives or no, this building must come down and down it will.

*(**MOTHER SUPERIOR** approaches her.)*

WALBURGA. She who is buried below shall not be disturbed.

MOTHER SUPERIOR. Give me the gun. You will not kill me.

WALBURGA. I will.

MOTHER SUPERIOR. No, you won't.

*(***TIMOTHY*** enters carrying his baseball bat.)*

TIMOTHY. Reverend Mother, we're about to start the baseball game. Could you give me a few last minute pointers?

MOTHER SUPERIOR. Timothy, darling, I'm somewhat occupied at the moment.

TIMOTHY. Why is Sister Maria Walburga pointing that gun at you?

WALBURGA. Because I am going to assassinate the heretic.

TIMOTHY. Oh no! You can't do that!

MOTHER SUPERIOR. Shhhh, Timothy. Everything is going to be all right. The Sister is merely overcome. *(to* **WALBURGA***)* Lissen, you over-cooked piece of Weiner Schnitzel, you don't have the guts to kill me.

JEREMY. Susan, don't taunt her. She's crazy.

MOTHER SUPERIOR. I know what I'm doing. It's psychology. I'm breaking down her defenses. You dried up dish of Sauerbraten; you soggy plate of strudel, you don't have the nerve to fire that gun. Look at your hands. They're shaking like an old woman. Go on, go on, shoot me, if you dare.

WALBURGA. I will! I will kill you.

TIMOTHY. Please, don't kill her.

MOTHER SUPERIOR. You shall not murder God's humble servant. Now, give me the gun.

*(She moves in closer to grab the gun. ***WALBURGA*** fires and ***MOTHER SUPERIOR*** is shot. ***JEREMY*** catches her fall. ***TIMOTHY*** screams.)*

WALBURGA. Joyce lives! *(***WALBURGA*** runs off.)*

ACACIUS. Somebody stop her! Marilyn! Carolyn! Harolyn! Attack! Stop that woman!

MOTHER SUPERIOR. Don't let them harm her. She must be forgiven.

JEREMY. She's getting away from them!

TIMOTHY. Over my dead body!

(ACACIUS tries to restrain him.)

MOTHER SUPERIOR. Timothy, you mustn't.

TIMOTHY. Let go. Reverend Mother, you're the only person in my entire life who has ever been kind to me.

ACACIUS. She's a vicious killer. You'll get hurt.

TIMOTHY. I'll show you I'm no sissy. I'll show you I'm a real man. I'll show you all! This is for you, Mother!

(TIMOTHY runs off.)

JEREMY. Someone call an ambulance!

MOTHER SUPERIOR. It's too late.

ACACIUS. *(looking out front)* Look! Timothy's caught up to her. Mother Machree, he's nabbed the kraut.

AGNES. He's tripped and tackled her. He's rubbing her face in the dirt.

MOTHER SUPERIOR. He's got her arms pinned back.

JEREMY. He's tying her up like a steer. What a kid.

ACACIUS. I sure as heck judged him wrong.

AGNES. Look over there. Who's that strange albino monk?

JEREMY. Whoever he is, the triplets have cut him off at the knees.

ACACIUS. Come on, girls. Get him in a half-nelson. Punch him in the gut. Yeah, you got him. Great gals.

MOTHER SUPERIOR. Who is that I see coming towards me? Sister Clarissa?

ACACIUS. Sister Clarissa died five years ago.

MOTHER SUPERIOR. Who is that with you? Oh my, it's Sister Helena. You're no longer in a wheelchair. You're walking.

ACACIUS. Sister Helena died ten years ago.

MOTHER SUPERIOR. How many of there are you? I can barely make out your faces. Of course, I'll go with you. Where are you taking me? To that beautiful golden light?

AGNES. Don't go to the light! Please, don't go!

JEREMY. I'm afraid there's nothing we can do to stop her.

ACACIUS. Yes, there is. Jeremy, move over. Agnes, go to your mother. Heal her.

AGNES. I can't. My powers are gone. Everything my voices told me was a lie. I am not the Immaculate Conception. I'm a bastard.

JEREMY. We're running out of time. You must try and save her.

AGNES. I can't!

MOTHER SUPERIOR. Ah, Sister Clotilde. Hello.

ACACIUS. Clotilde was always the last to show up anywhere. Reverend Mother's going fast. Please, I beg of you, Agnes. Heal her. I was an apostate. I didn't believe. I believe now. Heal her.

*(**MRS. LEVINSON** enters.)*

MRS. LEVINSON. What's happened?

JEREMY. She's been shot by a renegade Catholic hit woman. Doesn't look good.

MOTHER SUPERIOR. It is God's will.

MRS. LEVINSON. *(going for the Oscar)* How can it be God's will that you should be struck down by this maniac? All religion is a mania. I'm sick of it! Sick of it, I tell you. Down to the very last thread of my best Chanel suit. Every tragedy known to man derives from religious fanatics. If this be the hand of your merciful God, then I declare now that I am at war with Him. Damn me to Hell. I shall never forgive Him. Never!

AGNES. We must forgive to begin the healing.

*(**AGNES** gathers **MOTHER SUPERIOR** in her arms. She closes her eyes. Heavenly music is heard. **MOTHER SUPERIOR** sees a vision before her. She is radiant.)*

MOTHER SUPERIOR. Darling, is that you? Really? Oh, you don't have to say that, dear. Still, a wife does like to hear a compliment now and then.

ACACIUS. She's talking to the big boss.

MOTHER SUPERIOR. Now, Jesus, what's this about your having a sister? In all these years, I've never heard a word about her. Is this going to be a problem? All right. But look, when I get to Heaven don't spring on me your Cousin Irving.

AGNES. My Lord, please, do not take her this soon.

MOTHER SUPERIOR. Jesus, there's one more thing we need to clear up. What? What? Can't hear you. Say that again. What? What? Can't see you. Where are you? Sister Clarissa, did you see where Jesus went? Where are you going? Sister Helena, come back. Sister Clotilde? Hello? They've all gone.

JEREMY. And you're still here. Look, the wound is healed. There's no more blood.

ACACIUS. Agnes, you did it!

AGNES. *(disoriented)* What did I do?

MRS. LEVINSON. My darling granddaughter. I believe! *(like a black evangelist)* I BELIEVE!

JEREMY. *(to MOTHER SUPERIOR)* How do you feel?

MOTHER SUPERIOR. Never better. As if I had a restful night's sleep. More than anything, I feel a great need to sing.

MRS. LEVINSON. But you just barely escaped from the jaws of death.

MOTHER SUPERIOR. He hath blessed me with the gift of song and I must giveth back to the children. Acacius, gather them round.

ACACIUS. Sure thing, Reverend Mother.

(She runs off shouting "Children! Children! Get your asses over here!")

MOTHER SUPERIOR. Agnes, darling, would you be a dear and fetch my guitar?

AGNES. Of course. My pleasure.

MOTHER SUPERIOR. Mother Levinson, perhaps you should accompany her. The poor thing is still a little wobbly.

MRS. LEVINSON. Granddaughter, you lead. And like the Apostles, I shall follow.

(They exit. MOTHER SUPERIOR and JEREMY are alone.)

JEREMY. Well, we did it. We pulled it off. You were superb. An Oscar winning performance.

MOTHER SUPERIOR. I thank you. And you, you were marvelous as well. So convincing, I had to look down and make sure I wasn't really shot.

JEREMY. It couldn't have been easy filling Domino's gun with blanks.

MOTHER SUPERIOR. Yes, it took some clever maneuvering but once a crime reporter always a crime reporter. Oh, Jeremy, our daughter Agnes has regained her faith and that's all that matters. Jeremy, it's important to believe in miracles, even if you have to create them yourself.

JEREMY. You do work miracles and of that, I have no doubt. Will you at some point tell the others?

MOTHER SUPERIOR. Oh, I think it best we leave this a secret between – the three of us.

(ACACIUS, MRS. LEVINSON and AGNES return.)

ACACIUS. Children! Children, gather round.

MRS. LEVINSON. Yes, everyone, come closer.

(AGNES hands MOTHER SUPERIOR her guitar.)

AGNES. Here you are, Mother.

MOTHER SUPERIOR. My heart is so full. Full of love. Full of gratitude and full of song.

(She begins to sing and everyone joins in. Even SISTER WALBURGA aka Domino enters strapped into a straight jacket and joins them as their voices rise in rapturous song.)

LA, LA, LA, LA, LA, LA, LA, LA

A SONG WITHOUT WORDS
A MELODY FROM THE HEART
THREE NOTES FORM A CHORD
WHICH BRINGS US CLOSER TO THE LORD

THREE SIMPLE NOTES,
"LA, LA, LA"
A TRINITY OF HARMONY
SING HA-LAY-LOO-YAH!

LA, LA, LA, LA, LA, LA
LA, LA, LA, LA, LA, LA
LA, LA, LA. LA, LA, LA
LA, LA, LA, LA, LA, LA

A TRINITY OF HARMONY
SING HA-LAY-LOO-YAH!

End of Play

Also by
Charles Busch...

Die! Mommie! Die!
The Green Heart
The Lady in Question
Our Leading Lady
Psycho Beach Party
Queen Amarantha
Red Scare on Sunset
Shanghai Moon
Sleeping Beauty or Coma
The Tale of the Allergist's Wife
The Third Story
Times Square Angel
Vampire Lesbians of Sodom
You Should Be So Lucky

Please visit our website **samuelfrench.com** for complete
descriptions and licensing information.

OTHER TITLES AVAILABLE FROM SAMUEL FRENCH

VAMPIRE LESBIANS OF SODOM

Charles Busch

Farce / 6m, 2f / Unit Set

This truly bizarre entertainment of the *Rocky Horror* genre is about vamps, has nothing to do with lesbians and takes the audience from ancient Sodom to the Hollywood of the twenties and ends up in present day Las Vegas.

"Costumes flashier than pinball machines, outrageous lines, awful puns, sinister innocence, harmless depravity - it's all here. One can imagine a cult forming."
– *The New York Times*

"Bizarre and wonderful...If you think Boy George is a gender-bender, well, like Jolson said, you ain't seen nothing yet! Forget your genders, come on, get happy."
– *Broadway Magazine*

OTHER TITLES AVAILABLE FROM SAMUEL FRENCH

DIE! MOMMIE! DIE!

Charles Busch

Comic Melodrama / 3m, 3f / Interior

This comic melodrama evokes the 1960's movie thrillers that featured such aging cinematic icons as Bette Davis, Joan Crawford, Lana Turner and Susan Hayward. Faded pop singer, Angela Andrews, is trapped in a corrosive marriage to film producer, Sol Sussman. In her attempt to find happiness with her younger lover, an out of work TV star, Angela murders her husband with the aid of a poisoned suppository. In a plot that reflects both Greek tragedy as well as Hollywood folklore, Angela's resentful daughter, Edith, convinces Angela's emotionally disturbed son, Lance, to avenge their father's death by killing their mother. Lance, demanding proof of Angela's crime, slips some LSD into her after-dinner coffee, triggering a wild acid trip that exposes all of Angela's dark secrets.

812 B977

Busch, Charles.
The divine sister
Central Nonfiction CIRC -
2nd & 3rd fls
03/12